GUILTY!

by Diana G. Gallagher

illustrated by Brann Garvey

Librarian Reviewer
Laurie K. Holland
Media Specialist (National Board Certified), Edina, MN
MA in Elementary Education, Minnesota State University, Mankato

Reading Consultant
Elizabeth Stedem
Educator/Consultant, Colorado Springs, CO
MA in Elementary Education, University of Denver, CO

STONE ARCH BOOKS
MINNEAPOLIS   SAN DIEGO

Claudia Cristina Cortez is published by Stone Arch Books
151 Good Counsel Drive, P.O. Box 669
Mankato, Minnesota 56002
www.stonearchbooks.com

Library of Congress Cataloging-in-Publication Data
Gallagher, Diana G.
  Guilty!: The Complicated Life of Claudia Cristina Cortez / by Diana G.
Gallagher; illustrated by Brann Garvey.
  p. cm. — (Claudia Cristina Cortez)
  Summary: Thirteen-year-old Claudia learns about the American justice
system when, while studying for an American history quiz at Anna's house, she
and her friend Monica are accused of stealing ten dollars and their classmates
believe them to be guilty, based on circumstantial evidence.
  ISBN-13: 978-1-59889-838-5 (library binding)
  ISBN-10: 1-59889-838-8 (library binding)
  ISBN-13: 978-1-59889-881-1 (paperback)
  ISBN-10: 1-59889-881-7 (paperback)
  [1. Stealing—Fiction. 2. Justice—Fiction. 3. Middle schools—Fiction.
4. Schools—Fiction. 5. Contests—Fiction.] I. Garvey, Brann, ill. II. Title.
PZ7.G13543Gui 2008
[Fic]—dc22   2007005955

Art Director: Heather Kindseth
Graphic Designer: Kay Fraser

Photo Credits
Delaney Photography, cover

1 2 3 4 5 6 11 10 09 08 07 06

Table of Contents

Chapter 1
Even Luck 9

Chapter 2
Team Tactics 24

Chapter 3
Cash Crunch 34

Chapter 4
Big Trouble 40

Chapter 5
Goodbye, Viper Guy 45

Chapter 6
Missing Money Mystery 51

Chapter 7
The Canine Caper 56

Chapter 8
Cracking the Case 65

Chapter 9
The Quiz Show 70

Chapter 10
P.S. 76

Cast of

ME

CLAUDIA

That's me. I'm thirteen, and I'm in the seventh grade at Pine Tree Middle School. I live with my mom, my dad, and my brother, Jimmy. I have one cat, Ping-Ping. I like music, baseball, and hanging out with my friends.

MONICA is my very best friend. We met when we were really little, and we've been best friends ever since. I don't know what I'd do without her! Monica loves horses. In fact, when she grows up, she wants to be an Olympic rider!

MONICA

BECCA

BECCA is one of my closest friends. She lives next door to Monica. Becca is really, really smart. She gets good grades. She's also really good at art.

Characters

TOMMY's our class clown. Sometimes he's really funny, but sometimes he is just annoying. Becca has a crush on him . . . but I'd never tell.

I think **PETER** is probably the smartest person I've ever met. Seriously. He's even smarter than our teachers! He's also one of my friends. Which is lucky, because sometimes he helps me with homework.

ADAM and I met when we were in third grade. Now that we're teenagers, we don't spend as much time together as we did when we were kids, but he's always there for me when I need him. (Plus, he's the only person who wants to talk about baseball with me!)

Cast of

Every school has a bully, and **JENNY** is ours. She's the tallest person in our class, and the meanest, too. She always threatens to stomp people. No one's ever seen her stomp anyone, but that doesn't mean it hasn't happened!

ANNA is the most popular girl at our school. Everyone wants to be friends with her. I think that's weird, because Anna can be really, really mean. I mostly try to stay away from her.

CARLY is Anna's best friend. She always tries to act exactly like Anna does. She even wears the exact same clothes. She's never really been mean to me, but she's never been nice to me either!

Characters

NICK is my annoying seven-year-old neighbor. I get stuck babysitting him a lot. He likes to make me miserable. (Okay, he's not that bad ALL of the time . . . just most of the time.)

NICK

MS. STARK

MS. STARK teaches history, and she's also my homeroom teacher. She doesn't let us get away with much.

SYLVIA's nice, but we're not that close. She thinks Anna and Carly are so cool. She doesn't realize that they're mean.

SYLVIA

CHAPTER 1

EVEN LUCK

I have a lot of wishes.

Adults get to do a lot of the things I wish I could do. They get to drive, and go to bed whenever they want, and do a lot of other cool stuff I can't think of right now.

The **Claudia Cortez Wish List** is pretty long, but a Quiz Show about American history is not on it.

Unfortunately, I don't always get what I want. Especially in history class.

"What's a Quiz Show, Ms. Stark?" Carly asked.

"It's like *Jeopardy*, but about American history," our teacher replied.

My eyebrow arched. It does that when something sounds weird to me. American history? NOT FUN.

"It'll be fun," Ms. Stark said, "but there are some rules. Rule number one, no blurting out the answers. Each team will have a buzzer."

Like on TV game shows! Okay, so a Quiz Show might be a little fun.

"And no yelling," the teacher added.

Ms. Stark isn't WRINKLED and old like my grandma. She's just getting old. So she can still hear every little thing. It's amazing. Like she has superhero hearing or something. I never whisper secrets in Ms. Stark's class.

"I've split you up into teams. First, the Green Team," Ms. Stark said. "The first member is Claudia."

I held my breath and **crossed my fingers.** There were some kids I wanted on the Green Team with me, and a few I didn't.

"Monica and Becca," Ms. Stark went on.

That was great luck! I almost jumped out of my chair and whooped for joy, but I didn't.

I'm thirteen and in the seventh grade. I only jump and yell about things that are **totally awesome.**

Like if I got tickets to see Bad Dog, my all-time favorite band, next Saturday.

That's not going to happen, not in a gazillion years, but I'd jump for joy if it did.

Anyway, Monica has been my best friend since the first day of kindergarten. She loves horses and almost always goes along with my **wild ideas.** Plus, if something goes wrong, she doesn't get mad.

That's good. A lot of my ideas don't work out the way I planned.

My second best friend, Becca, likes to draw and make jewelry. She tries to talk Monica and me out of our really crazy ideas.

If we won't listen, Becca goes home. Sometimes **she misses out on a lot of fun,** but mostly she **stays out of trouble.**

If Becca and Monica were around, bad times weren't so bad.

Just as I decided the Quiz Show might be fun after all, the **bad luck** happened to even out my GOOD LUCK.

I have what my dad calls "even luck." Sometimes I have good luck, but sometimes I have bad luck. So it evens out. It evened out this time, too.

"Carly and Anna," Ms. Stark said.

"What?!" I gasped. Then I covered my mouth, but it was too late. Everyone had heard me.

Ms. Stark thought I hadn't heard her. "Carly and Anna are the other people on the Green Team," she said again.

Anna is the most popular girl in Pine Tree Middle School. I don't know why. She's a SNOB and she's BOSSY, and nobody really likes her. Except Carly.

Carly is Anna's best friend. She copies everything Anna says and does. I think she even has all matching clothes. It's **creepy.**

Ms. Stark put my other best friend, Adam, on the Blue Team with Peter.

Peter is the smartest kid in the whole school, **including the eighth graders.** He doesn't talk much, except when he's answering questions. He knows the answers to everything.

After Ms. Stark finished picking the teams, she gave us more bad news.

"Each Quiz Show team will be graded," Ms. Stark explained. "Poor, fair, good, or excellent."

Aha! The Quiz Show was a trick to make us learn.

1. Nobody wanted to look lame in front of the whole class.

2. So we had to know the answers.

3. That meant we had to study.

The Quiz Show was just like a test, but not in writing. Teachers can be so sneaky.

"The Quiz Show will take place on Friday. Your team will have this week to study together and practice. Your grades will be based on getting questions right, working as a team, and how well you follow the rules," Ms. Stark said. "And I'd like each team to choose a captain."

Uh-oh. That was a problem.

Anna would want to be captain of the Green Team. We'd have to do everything her way, even if it wasn't the best way. There would be no point arguing about it.

If Anna wasn't the captain, she might:

A. Decide not to answer anything.

B. Hog all the questions.

C. Fake being sick so she didn't have to come to school on Friday.

Anna doesn't care about consequences when she's MAD.

Consequences are what happen because something else happened. If my dad got me tickets to go see Bad Dog because I did the dishes all week without being asked, that would be a GOOD CONSEQUENCE.

Usually people only care about bad consequences. Like when I was grounded one weekend because I didn't clean my room.

I started to pick up the mess on Monday, but then I got busy. **I am a teenager, after all.**

The next thing I knew it was Friday, and the whole week was over!

I got grounded. That was a bad consequence.

I sure didn't expect to hear good news about the Quiz Show. But Ms. Stark wasn't done telling us about it yet.

Ms. Stark explained that the teams would get points for correct answers. Then she smiled. "There's a PRIZE for the winning team," she said. "I went to college with the lead singer of Bad Dog, and . . ."

Everyone GASPED.

Ms. Stark went on, "He has given me some free tickets to the concert next week. So each person on the winning team will win **two free tickets.**"

I jumped out of my chair and yelled, **"Yay!"**

* * *

I'm not thrilled about being on a Quiz Show team with Anna and Carly. They are very annoying.

It's not just that Anna wants her own way, or that Carly lets her have it. They act like everyone should be thrilled if they say hi.

At least I wasn't on the same team as Jenny Pinski. That would be a hundred times **WORSE**.

No, a thousand times worse.

It would be a disaster!

I'm not kidding.

Jenny is big and mean. At lunch, she made the whole Red Team sit with her. **Nobody had the guts to refuse.**

Adam and I were sitting at the next table. He had some baseball cards spread out next to his tray. We're both huge fans of the Harmon County Hawks. Baseball is in the Top Ten on my list of FAVORITE THINGS. That's one reason Adam and I are friends.

Anyway, we heard everything at Jenny's table.

"We better **not lose** the Quiz Show," Jenny said. "I want those concert tickets."

The other kids on the Red Team stared at Jenny. They were too scared to speak.

"I don't want to **look stupid,** either. So you better let me answer some of the questions. Or else." Jenny frowned meanly.

All the kids on the Red Team nodded. They looked SCARED.

"I'm glad I'm not on the Red Team," Adam whispered.

"Me too," I whispered back.

When Jenny says "or else" she means, **"Or else I'll stomp you."** She's been saying that for years. I can't think of one time Jenny ever stomped anyone, but nobody wants to be first.

When we got to fifth period English, I thought it would be me!

My friends are in most of my classes. We have Ms. Stark for homeroom and history. Mrs. Sanchez teaches fifth period English, my WORST class of the day.

Don't get me wrong. Reading and writing are my favorite things to do in school. But in English class, I have to sit next to Jenny.

It's hard to concentrate when you're a nervous wreck. **Anything could happen!**

Yesterday we read a story during class. Today we had to answer workbook questions about it. I was on the third question when everything went **kablooey.**

(KABLOOEY isn't a real word. My grandma uses it to describe disasters. Like when she set the timer wrong and a potato blew up in the microwave.)

Out of the blue, Jenny raised her hand. "Claudia stole my pencil, Mrs. Sanchez."

I looked up. I was so SHOCKED that I forgot to be scared. "I did not," I said.

"Yes, you did." Jenny glared at me.

I glared back. "I **did not** take your pencil."

"Then why is it in your backpack?" Jenny pointed down.

I looked down at my backpack. A blue pencil was sticking out of the side pocket. It wasn't mine. All my pencils are yellow.

"You shouldn't be so quick to blame someone, Jenny," Mrs. Sanchez said.

"Yeah," Monica said. "There's no way Claudia did it."

Monica was right about that. I'm IMPULSIVE and sometimes I talk too much, but **I'm not a fool.** There's no way I'd have taken Jenny's pencil! She was accusing me of **a crime I didn't do!**

"But my pencil is in Claudia's backpack," Jenny said.

"Sometimes evidence doesn't prove that a crime happened," Mrs. Sanchez said.

Everyone stared at her with BLANK FACES.

"There are three parts to every crime," the teacher explained. "**Opportunity, means,** and **motive.**"

Our faces stayed blank.

"In other words," Mrs. Sanchez continued, "was Claudia in a position to commit the crime? Did she have the opportunity?"

"Claudia is sitting right there!" Jenny yelled. She glared at me again.

I groaned.

"Did the accused person have the means, or the ability, to commit the crime?" Mrs. Sanchez added.

Jenny rolled her eyes. "It's not hard to pick up a pencil and drop it in a backpack. **Claudia has hands.**"

Several kids giggled. I didn't think it was funny.

"The pencil could have rolled off Jenny's desk and fallen into Claudia's backpack," Adam said. "That's not stealing. That's an **accident.**"

"Finally, did the accused person have a motive, a reason to commit the crime?" Mrs. Sanchez asked.

"Claudia has a perfectly good pencil," Monica pointed out. "It isn't even halfway down to the eraser."

"I also have four new pencils," I said. I reached into my backpack and pulled out four unsharpened yellow pencils.

"That proves Claudia didn't do it," Becca said. "She doesn't need a pencil."

"Plus, nobody saw Claudia do it," Adam said. "There aren't any witnesses."

"That's right, Adam," Mrs. Sanchez said. "The evidence is CIRCUMSTANTIAL. Circumstantial evidence makes the accused person look guilty but doesn't prove it."

Then Mrs. Sanchez said, "All we know is that somehow, the pencil ended up in Claudia's bag. **That makes her look guilty, but does not prove that she took it.** So we have reasonable doubt."

"What's **reasonable doubt?**" Carly asked.

"That means there are very good reasons to think the accused person did not commit the crime," Mrs. Sanchez said.

I started to feel better. My friends had come to my defense, and there was no HARD EVIDENCE against me.

Still, my trial wasn't over yet.

"All right, class," Mrs. Sanchez said. "You've just heard all the evidence. Now we need a verdict. How many of you think **Claudia is innocent?**"

Everyone in the class raised a hand.

Except Jenny.

"Do you really think Claudia took your pencil, Jenny?" Mrs. Sanchez asked.

Jenny shrugged. "Maybe she did and maybe she didn't. We'll never know."

As I said before, there are worse things than being on a Quiz Show team with Anna and Carly.

That wasn't the first time I almost went down in Pine Tree Middle School history as the **first person Jenny Pinski stomped.**

And it wouldn't be the last.

CHAPTER 2

TEAM TACTICS

Anna decided that the Green Team should practice for the Quiz Show **every day**. We all walked to her house after school.

On the walk to Anna's, we talked about our strategy to **WIN** the Quiz Show.

"We need books with questions about American history," Anna said.

"Books with questions and answers," Carly added.

"I'll look online," Becca offered.

"My dad has an American history trivia book we could borrow," I said.

Anna frowned. "But **knowing the answers won't be enough to win,**" she said.

"Why not?" Carly asked. "That's how we get points."

"But we can't answer if we don't hit the buzzer first," Anna explained. "We should practice that, too."

"I think Anna should be the team captain," Carly said.

"That's fine with me," I said. I REALLY wanted those Bad Dog concert tickets. So far, Anna had good ideas about how to win.

"Get in line, people!" Anna suddenly snapped. She sounded **just like Ms. Stark** on a field trip.

I didn't jump to obey her. **I don't like being ordered around** by other people, especially **people my age.**

Then I saw why Anna wanted us to line up. Sylvia was walking ahead of us.

Sylvia is nice, but she does everything in slow motion. She pauses between words when she talks, and she takes forever to go anywhere.

Most kids GOBBLE dessert so fast they don't taste it. Sylvia **nibbles** and **tastes** every tiny bite.

She should have come with a remote. Then we could **fast-forward** her up to normal speed.

Sylvia smiled and waved as we marched past her one by one.

I smiled and waved back.

"I'm glad Sylvia isn't on our team," Carly said.

I looked back over my shoulder. Sylvia was far behind us. She couldn't hear what Carly was saying about her.

"Me too," Anna agreed. "Sylvia talks so slowly **she might not finish her answers** before time ran out."

We only had thirty seconds to answer each question.

"Sylvia can't help it," Becca said. "That's just the way she is."

Anna grinned. "And it's the White Team's **problem.**"

"The Red Team has a bigger problem," I said. I told them what Jenny had said at lunch.

"So **Jenny will be mad if her team loses,**" Monica said. "And mad if the other kids don't let her answer questions."

"Right," I said. "So they'll probably lose. **Jenny** doesn't know everything. Peter does."

"Well, that's a problem for us," Anna said. "Peter gives the Blue Team a **huge advantage.**"

Just then Tommy ran in front of us. He stopped, turned around, and made a **disgusting noise.**

"Is that supposed to be funny, Tommy?" Anna asked.

"We're **not laughing,**" Monica said.

Tommy is the class clown. He thinks everything he does is 𝓗𝓘𝓛𝓐𝓡𝓘𝓞𝓤𝓢, but sometimes he can be really **annoying.** He laughed loudly, and then ran off down the street.

"Maybe the Blue Team won't be that hard to beat," I said, rolling my eyes. "Tommy might cancel out the Peter advantage."

"I hope so!" Anna exclaimed. "If we don't win the Bad Dog tickets, I'll have to use my allowance money to buy a ticket. **I wanted to use that money for the book fair.**"

The book fair was taking place Friday afternoon in the library. It's one of my favorite things at school. It only happens once a year.

"I have ten dollars saved so far," Anna said. She opened her shoulder bag and unzipped an inside pocket. She pulled out a five-dollar bill and five ones.

"I want to buy the new **Debra Doyle, Teen Detective** book," she said. "It just came out. I saw it on the Internet."

"A concert ticket costs a lot more than ten dollars," I pointed out.

"My dad said he would help me pay for it, but I had to choose." Anna put the money back in the zipped pocket. "I can get the book that I want. Or I can chip in to help pay for a **Bad Dog ticket.** I already have their CD, so I decided to get the book. **But if I can get both, I will.**"

At least Anna's father gave her a choice. My dad said he wouldn't spend his money on music that hurts his ears.

He said, "Don't bother begging."

"I won't have to choose if we win the Quiz Show," Anna said. "I'll buy my book, and I'll have two tickets."

"I'll have four!" Carly exclaimed. "My mom already bought two tickets for me."

Carly is an only child, and she's really spoiled. Her parents get her almost EVERYTHING she wants.

Winning the Quiz Show was my only hope of seeing Bad Dog in person.

* * *

Anna paused when we stepped inside her kitchen. She hung her sweater and backpack on a hook by the door. **She had to stand on her tiptoes to reach the lower pegs.**

I wondered why the hooks were so high.

"Is everyone else in your family tall, Anna?"
I asked.

"Just the boys," Anna's older brother said.

Ben and his friend Max walked into the kitchen right behind us.

Ben is seventeen, a junior at Pine Tree High, and tall. He did not have to stand on his tiptoes to hang his jacket on a top peg. **Max is even taller!**

"Max and I are going to play SERPENT'S REVENGE in my room," Ben said. "Don't bug us."

"We finally reached the last level," Max said.

"We aren't here to play games, Ben," Anna said. "We have to study." She waved the Green Team to follow her.

Ben and Max walked down the hall ahead of us.

"I'm buying the new **Viper Man** game next Saturday," Ben said. "After I get paid for mowing lawns."

"I've got money saved," Max said. "But I need new basketball shoes, and they cost over a hundred dollars."

I wasn't spying on them. Sometimes, boys talk really loudly.

Anna led the Green Team into her room and closed the door.

I sat on the bed with Monica and Becca. Anna sat at her desk. Carly flopped on a pillow on the floor.

"I need more money, too," Becca said. "For the Book Fair."

"What books do you want?" I asked.

"I just want one," Becca said. "But it's a big book called How To Draw Everything. I'm three dollars short."

"I don't have enough money for the books I want, either." I sighed.

Then I perked up. "But the Book Fair isn't until Friday. **We have four days to earn more.**"

"No, you don't," Anna said. "You'll be too busy studying for the Quiz Show."

I could study and earn money, but I just shrugged. I didn't want to argue with Anna. **Arguing would wreck our team spirit.**

"Before we get started, can I use your bathroom?" I asked.

Anna sighed. "Fine. It's down the hall," she said.

When I came back, Anna had a great idea.

"We don't have a lot of time," Anna reminded us. "Instead of everyone studying everything, we should each study a different part of American history."

"Then we'll all be experts on a few topics!" Monica exclaimed. "That's 𝔹ℝ𝕀𝕃𝕃𝕀𝔸ℕ𝕋, Anna!"

Even I was **impressed.** I picked the American Revolution and the Constitution.

"Can I get a drink of water?" Becca asked.

"Sure," Anna said. "In the kitchen."

Becca came back just as Carly decided to take the Civil War. **Carly wasn't interested in the Old West.** Anna said she had to study the whole second half of the 1800s anyway.

Anna took everything before the American Revolution.

"What's left?" Becca asked.

"The twentieth century," Monica said.

"I'll take the first fifty years," Becca said.

"And I'll do the rest," Monica said. She looked at her watch. "Can I use your phone, Anna? I have to call my mom."

"There's a phone in the kitchen," Anna said. **She rolled her eyes.** "My parents won't let me have one in my room until I'm in high school."

"That's okay, Anna," I said. "You won't have time to talk on the phone. **You'll be too busy studying for the Quiz Show.**"

CHAPTER 3

CASH CRUNCH

Nicholas Wright is at the top of my **Things I Can't Stand list,** right above cooked cauliflower and getting **shots.** He's the seven-year-old BRAT that lives next door.

Nick was at my house when I got home.

"You smell funny, Claudia." Nick made a face and a DISGUSTING **noise**.

I wanted to say that he had big ears or tell him to get lost, but I have better manners. Besides, **insults don't bother Nick.**

"Where's your mother?" I asked.

"I don't know." Nick frowned and folded his arms. "You have to play with me."

"Don't think so," I said. Then I yelled, "MOM!"

When Mom's not working, she watches Nick. For free! She wants to be a good neighbor. **I usually get stuck watching him, though.** She would never admit it, but **I don't think my mother can stand Nick either.**

Mom stuck her head out the laundry room door. "Mrs. Wright will be home soon, Claudia. Watch Nick until then, okay?"

"Okay," I said with a sigh.

I was officially babysitting.

Sometimes I whine and try to get out of babysitting. Nick is loud, never stops moving, and he's always doing something he shouldn't. **It isn't exactly fun to watch him.**

This time I didn't complain. Mom pays me two dollars an hour. That money would help me get my books at the book fair.

"Told ya!" Nick yelled. He drew his foot back to kick me.

I jumped back, and **he missed.**

During the next thirty minutes, **Nick pulled my hair, spilled orange juice, threw a temper tantrum, locked himself in the bathroom, and tried to smash my antique china doll.**

I was exhausted when Mrs. Wright finally took Nick home. Half an hour of Nick duty is **worth a lot more than a dollar.** But it's the only income I can count on.

I asked if Mrs. Wright needed me to watch Nick again before Friday. She didn't.

That was **good for my nerves** but bad for my finances.

My parents don't pay my brother, Jimmy, and me to do chores. **It's our duty to help out the family.**

I'd wrestle Jenny Pinski before I'd ask my dad for a loan. He doesn't approve of borrowing.

Jimmy makes money mowing lawns in our neighborhood. He spends most of his money on video games. He spends the rest on comics. I went to his room after dinner.

Jimmy thinks I'm annoying. **He hardly ever talks to me unless he wants something.** But I knew that he still wanted my special edition comic for his collection.

"Do you still want to buy my **mint condition Viper Man double issue number 3?**" I asked.

"How much?" Jimmy asked.

"Seven dollars," I said. It was a hard comic book to find, and it was in perfect condition. Seven dollars was a fair price.

"No, thanks," Jimmy said. "I can get it online for five dollars."

I was running out of ways to make money. I had to think of something.

Dad said I was too young to work in his computer store.

Mom said she wasn't going to pay me three dollars an hour for babysitting.

I was feeling really FRUSTRATED. I went outside.

Mr. and Mrs. Gomez live across the street.

Mr. Gomez was outside watering the grass. He likes golf so much he turned his front yard into a putting green. He's retired and doesn't have anything else to do.

I smiled as I crossed the street.

"Hi, Mr. Gomez!" I called.

Mr. Gomez smiled back. "Good evening, Claudia."

"Do you have any jobs I could do?" I asked. I stayed on the sidewalk.

Mr. Gomez is very nice, except when someone messes up his lawn. I was CAREFUL not to walk on it.

"Well, let's see," Mr. Gomez said, rubbing his chin.

"I'm trying to earn money to buy books," I added. Sometimes adults will make up errands to help pay for educational things like books and field trips.

"Hi, Claudia!" Mrs. Gomez said, walking out of the house with her little dog, Fancy.

The poodle started yapping as soon as it saw me.

Mr. Gomez looked at me and said, "I'll give you five dollars to walk Fancy, Claudia."

"Okay!" I said. **I jumped at the chance.**

The only time Mr. and Mrs. Gomez fight is when Mrs. Gomez's dog goes to the bathroom on their lawn. That only happens when Mrs. Gomez is **too tired** to walk Fancy.

"Thank you, but we don't need you to do that today, Claudia," Mrs. Gomez said. "I'd like to walk Fancy myself."

I watched **five dollars on four legs** prance away up the street.

Suddenly, earning seven dollars by Friday seemed **IMPOSSIBLE**.

CHAPTER 4

BIG TROUBLE

I took my dad's American history trivia book to school the next day. Everyone on the Green Team sat at the same table for lunch.

"This is a **fantastic** book, Claudia!" Monica exclaimed. "It's even divided into topics."

"Ask me something about the Great Depression," Becca said.

"Okay. Then you ask me about Abraham Lincoln," Carly said. "He was the president during the Civil War."

Anna didn't want to practice. **She was mad.**

"One of you is in big trouble," Anna said.

We all blinked.

"What for?" Carly asked.

"Not you, Carly," Anna said. She glared at Monica, Becca, and me. "One of them."

"What did we do?" I asked.

"My ten dollars is gone," Anna said. "And one of you took it."

My mouth fell open. Monica and Becca looked shocked and surprised too.

Anna had just accused my friends and me of committing a real crime. **Stealing money was way worse than taking a pencil.**

"Why do you think one of us took it, Anna?" I asked.

"I've read a lot of detective books," Anna said. "It wasn't that hard to figure out."

"I can't wait to hear," Carly said. She looked relieved because Anna didn't suspect her.

"First," Anna began, "I didn't show my SECRET money pocket to anyone else. And second, each one of you left my bedroom yesterday. Alone."

OPPORTUNITY, I thought. Just like Ms. Sanchez said.

"You had time to go to the kitchen and take the money out of my bag," Anna continued.

And the MEANS, I realized.

"And you all need more money for the Book Fair," Anna finished.

"They all have MOTIVES!" Carly exclaimed.

"Right," Anna agreed.

"That doesn't mean **one of us is guilty**," I said.

"Yeah," Monica chimed in. "Carly could have done it."

"Carly didn't leave my room, and she doesn't need money," Anna explained. **"Carly gets a huge allowance."**

"And my parents buy all the books I want," Carly added.

"Well, my mom paid me to dust and vacuum yesterday," Becca said. "I earned the money I need for my art book."

"And she can prove it," I said.

Becca had an adult witness. She was in the clear.

"I have twelve dollars," Monica said.

"The White Pony book only costs eight dollars," I said.

"I have to buy my little sister a **birthday present** instead," Monica explained. "She wants a Merry Mermaid sea horse play set."

"Do you have enough for your books, Claudia?" Carly asked.

"No," I answered honestly.

"That's why you and Monica are my biggest SUSPECTS," Anna concluded.

"But we didn't do it!" I protested.

I knew I was innocent, and Monica would never steal.

Then I remembered what Mrs. Sanchez told us yesterday. "All your evidence is **circumstantial.** That's not good enough," I said.

"Sure it is," Anna said. **"TV cops arrest people because of circumstantial evidence all the time."**

I imagined the police showing up at my house to arrest me.

I didn't want to go to jail!

CHAPTER 5

GOODBYE, VIPER GUY

Monica and Becca came to my backyard after school and joined me in Jimmy's old tree house.

"We have a **huge problem,**" I said.

"Yeah," Monica agreed. "I can't believe Anna thinks we stole from her."

"And Carly is a 𝔹𝕃𝔸𝔹𝔹𝔼ℝ𝕄𝕆𝕌𝕋ℍ," I added. "By tomorrow, everyone at Pine Tree Middle School will know about it."

"I bet they already know," Becca said. "You have to prove you didn't do it."

"How?" I asked.

"I'm not going to buy the White Pony book at the Book Fair," Monica said. "If you don't buy your books, won't that prove **we didn't take Anna's money?**"

"I don't think so," I said. "That would only prove we're too smart to spend stolen money at school."

"Oh, yeah." Monica sighed. "It would look like we're just laying low."

"Waiting for things to blow over," I said.

Monica gasped. "Everyone will think we're THIEVES until we graduate!"

"No, they won't," I said.

I sounded more positive than I felt, because Monica needed some **serious cheering up.**

I told her, "I'll think of some way to prove that we didn't do it. Promise."

My dad says **every problem has a solution.** He's probably right, but I didn't have a clue how to solve ours.

There wasn't even time to think about it. I had to do homework and cram more history facts into my brain. The Green Team still had a chance to win.

Of course, winning the Quiz Show wouldn't be much fun if everyone thought I was a CROOK.

Here's a word of advice. Don't ever think that things could be worse. Every time I think that, things get worse.

Right after Monica and Becca left, I got stuck watching Nick. My mom wanted to finish cleaning so I had to watch Nick at his house.

I tried to look on the bright side. Nick's mom would be gone an hour, so my mom would pay me two dollars. Then I'd only need five dollars more to buy my three books.

However, being around Nick is always AWFUL.

He didn't want to watch cartoons or play a video game. He wanted to beat the babysitter at hide-and-seek, Go Fish, and tackle tag.

When I got home, I felt like I'd been trampled, chewed up, and spit out by a T-Rex.

Then things got worse again!

Five minutes after I walked in my front door, Nick and his mother came over.

"Do you know what happened to Nick's **Viper Man action figure,** Claudia?" Mrs. Wright asked.

"Claudia took it!" Nick cried. He pointed at me. "So she has to buy me a new one."

"I did not steal your Viper Man, Nick!" I couldn't believe it. I had been **falsely accused** of theft twice in two days!

"Mrs. Wright doesn't think you stole Nick's toy," my mother said.

"Of course not," Mrs. Wright said. "I thought maybe you took Viper Man to make Nick behave. Then you just FORGOT to give it back."

"I didn't take it at all," I said. "Honestly. But I'll help look for it."

I followed Nick and his mom back to their house.

What would a real detective do? I wondered.

The answer was easy. A real detective would start looking in the place where the victim was last seen.

I went straight to Nick's room.

I took everything out of Nick's toy box, but Viper Man wasn't in it. The action figure wasn't in Nick's closet or dresser drawers, either.

Then I looked under the bed.

I saw something small and suspicious. It looked like a tiny foot. It was attached to a tiny plastic leg. It was not attached to a Viper Man.

"What's this, Nick?" I held up the plastic leg.

"I don't know." Nick didn't look me in the eye.

In the garage, I found the rest of the toy. Nick's Viper Man was in a trashcan. He only had one leg.

"Did you break your toy?" Mrs. Wright asked Nick. "And blame Claudia so you could get a new one?"

Nick scrunched his face in a furious frown. He folded his arms and wouldn't answer, but it didn't matter.

The evidence proved two things.

1. Nick was guilty of breaking the toy.

2. He was also guilty of lying about it.

"You are in BIG TROUBLE, young man," Mrs. Wright said. "And you will be punished, as soon as your father gets home."

I didn't feel sorry for Nick. He had caused me a lot of trouble.

At least my luck had started to even out.

Mrs. Wright knew I didn't take Nick's Viper Man. And the police hadn't shown up at my house to arrest me for taking Anna's money.

Even better, solving the Case of the Missing Plastic Person gave me a fantastic idea!

There was one way to prove that Monica and I didn't take Anna's money.

I had to find out who did.

MISSING MONEY MYSTERY

I saw a detective on TV once who kept track of her case notes in a small electronic organizer.

I used a small notebook with pages marked for witnesses, suspects, and evidence.

I took it to school on Wednesday.

Taking money out of a shoulder bag is easy. Anyone who was in Anna's house on Monday night or Tuesday morning could have done it. That wouldn't help me find the REAL THIEF.

But maybe Monica, Becca, and I weren't the only people who had the OPPORTUNITY to take Anna's money.

Part One of my plan was simple. I had to question the witnesses. Anna was at the top of the list.

I found Anna in the girl's room between classes.

"The **prime suspect** isn't supposed to question the 𝒱𝐼𝒞𝒯𝐼𝑀, Claudia," Anna said. She sounded annoyed.

I asked my questions anyway. "When did you find out that your money was **missing?**"

"Tuesday morning," Anna answered. "When I left for school."

"So 𝒜𝒩𝒴𝒪𝒩𝐸 who was in your house from Monday afternoon until yesterday morning could have taken your money," I said.

"My parents and my brother?" Anna laughed. "**My mom and dad don't need my money.** Neither does Ben. He makes lots of money mowing lawns."

Anna didn't help me solve the case, but Becca and Monica were witnesses, too.

At lunch, I kept trying to crack the case.

"Did you see anyone else in Anna's kitchen on Monday afternoon?" I asked.

"Sorry, Claudia." Becca shook her head.

"I didn't see anyone," Monica said, "but maybe Carly did. **She was still there when we left.**"

"That's right, she was!" I exclaimed.

I didn't think Carly was guilty. She didn't need the money. Even if she did, she wouldn't steal from Anna. But she might have seen something important.

I looked around the cafeteria. Carly was at a corner table, waiting for Anna. I walked over and sat down.

"That seat's taken," Carly said.

"I won't be here long," I said.

Anna walked over and set her lunch tray on the table. "Stop bugging my friends, Claudia."

"Just one question," I said. "Did you see anyone in Anna's kitchen after we left Monday, Carly?"

Carly tilted her head and squinted. **Then her eyes widened.** "You know what? I did see someone," she said.

"Who?" Anna looked surprised.

"Ben's friend, Max," Carly said. "He was getting a **soda** out of the fridge."

"That doesn't mean Max took my money," Anna said.

"No, it doesn't," I agreed.

"I just can't believe he would," Anna said. Then she frowned. **She was quiet** for a long moment.

"What?" I asked.

"I just remembered," Anna said. "I had to stand on a chair to get my shoulder bag down yesterday morning."

My eyebrow arched. "From the bottom peg?" I asked.

Anna shook her head. "No. It was hanging on a top peg."

Monday afternoon, Anna had to stand on tiptoe to hang her bag on a bottom peg. **She couldn't reach the top pegs.** But Max was really tall.

"Max can't be guilty," Carly said. "He's a STAR on the Pine Tree High basketball team!"

I didn't want to believe it, either. Max was in Anna's kitchen, and he needed money to buy new basketball shoes. But that was **circumstantial evidence** like Anna had against Monica and me. It wasn't hard evidence.

On TV, detectives weren't allowed to accuse anyone unless they could PROVE the suspect had committed the crime.

If Max was the thief, I had to prove it.

But how?

CHAPTER 7

THE CANINE CAPER

Adam stopped me on the sidewalk after school. "Want to help me practice pitching, Claudia?" He held up his baseball mitt and a ball.

"I can't today," I said. "Between homework and the Quiz Show and trying to figure out who took Anna's money, I'm just too busy."

"Do you have any clues?" Adam asked.

"Yeah," I admitted, "but I need more **evidence.**"

"Well, **I know you and Monica didn't do it**," Adam said. "Do you need any help?"

"No, but thanks," I said.

I didn't know what would happen in **Part Two** of my plan.

That's because my plan didn't have a Phase
Two yet.

When I got home, Mr. Gomez waved me over to his
yard. His face was red, and he SPIT when he talked.

"Look at this, Claudia!" The old man opened his
pooper-scooper.

It was full of doggie doo!

"Gross!" I said. It was DISGUSTING.

"I've picked up a mess every morning for the
past three days." Mr. Gomez snarled. Really. I'm
not making it up. I've never seen him so mad! His
lawn is really important to him.

"It can't be from Fancy," I said. "It's too big."

Mr. Gomez leaned over to look me in the eye.
**"Find the dog that's using my yard for a toilet,
and I'll give you a ten-dollar reward."**

"Wow! Okay!" I exclaimed.

If I had Mr. Gomez's reward, I could buy
THREE BOOKS and have money left over!

I wanted to tackle the **Whose Dog Did It Mystery**, but it was more important to solve the **Case of Anna's Missing Money.**

Otherwise, no one would ever believe that Monica and I were INNOCENT. Except Adam and Becca, of course.

I told Mr. Gomez I'd keep an eye out for the dog. Then I went home and went into my brother's room. Jimmy works at Dad's computer store on Wednesday afternoons, so I knew he wouldn't be home.

I used Jimmy's computer and found the Pine Tree High School website. I clicked on SPORTS and then on **basketball.**

Max Cooper was a guard on the Pine Tree Eagles varsity team. They were playing a home game on Friday.

I didn't know if the new information would help. I couldn't do anything about it until the next day anyway.

The Quiz Show was only two days away, and I had to **study like crazy** if I wanted those concert tickets.

Going to the Bad Dog concert would either:

A. Make me feel better if I was depressed because everyone still thought I was thief

OR

B. Make my celebration better because everyone knew I was innocent.

Either way, I wanted to win **the tickets.**

* * *

I couldn't sleep Wednesday night. I had too much on my mind.

My parents wouldn't let me watch TV, so I watched Mr. Gomez's lawn from my bedroom window. My room is on the second floor, so I had a good view.

After a few minutes, Mr. Gomez walked outside. I guess he couldn't sleep either.

He was guarding his yard with his trusty pooper-scooper. After half an hour, he went inside.

I still wasn't tired, so I kept watching.

Fifteen minutes later, a big brown dog with a white spot on its head stopped on Mr. Gomez's grass.

The dog wasn't on a leash or with a person.

The dog did its nasty business. Then it ran back up the street.

"Hmm," I said to myself. "I think I've cracked the case."

* * *

The next morning, I got up early. I walked over to Mr. Gomez's house, **scooped the dog's mess into a plastic grocery bag,** and threw it away.

I didn't want Mr. Gomez to get mad again. It's not healthy, especially for old people.

Then I left to find the **guilty dog.**

I have a cat, but almost everyone else in my neighborhood has a dog. Some people have two or three.

Most of the dogs stay outside in fenced yards.

They all bark when someone walks by, even the dogs that stay inside. **They can see out the windows.**

The brown dog with the white spot lived on the next block. The backyard wasn't fenced so the dog wasn't outside. I saw it through the front window.

I walked up to the porch, thought up an excuse, and knocked.

A woman opened the door. Her brown hair was turning gray, and her leg was in a cast. "May I help you?" she asked.

I almost choked! Then I found my undercover detective voice.

"My name is Claudia," I said. "I live over on the next block. Your dog was over by my house last night. I just wanted to make sure he got home okay."

"Yes, he did." The woman sighed. "I am so sorry."

I glanced at a magazine on the table by the door. It was addressed to **Mrs. Joan Arnold.** I had found the dog's owner and I knew her name.

Mr. Gomez's reward was mine.

"My son has been walking Buster since I broke my foot," Mrs. Arnold said. "But he's been out of town."

I realized that Mrs. Arnold wasn't letting Buster run loose because she was LAZY.

She had a broken foot and couldn't walk him.

"I know I shouldn't let Buster out alone," Mrs. Arnold said. "But my son won't be back until Tuesday."

I suddenly wished I wasn't such a good detective. I didn't want to tell Mr. Gomez about Buster. Not even to get a ten-dollar REWARD.

Mr. Gomez might call the police. Then the police might take Buster away. They might even **arrest** Mrs. Arnold for breaking the leash laws!

"Buster hasn't done anything terrible," I said. "Except for leaving a **MESS** on Mr. Gomez's lawn."

"Oh, dear," Mrs. Arnold said. She looked very upset. "Mr. Gomez takes such good care of his lawn.

"He won't stay mad if Buster doesn't go on his lawn anymore," I said. "I don't even have to tell him it was your dog. **I'll walk Buster until your son gets back.**"

Mrs. Arnold hired me on the spot. She even paid me ten dollars in advance for not ratting out Buster to Mr. Gomez.

I felt **great** as I headed for school. Mrs. Arnold's ten dollars was more than I needed to buy my three books.

But it didn't solve my problem.

I still couldn't **PROVE** that I hadn't stolen Anna's money.

I had to solve the **Case of Anna's Missing Money.**

I had to clear my name and Monica's.

I only had one suspect.

MAX.

CHAPTER 8

CRACKING THE CASE

After school on Thursday, Monica and I walked to the high school for **Part Two** of my plan. We hid in the bushes by the gym doors to wait. The basketball team was practicing for their game on Friday.

"What are we doing here?" Monica asked.

"We're on a STAKE-OUT," I explained. I didn't know if spying on Max would prove he took Anna's money or not, but it was the only thing I could think of.

When the players rushed out of the school after practice, **Monica started to giggle.**

I shushed her. "Quit it, Monica! Good detectives don't giggle!"

"I can't help it, Claudia," Monica said. "**I giggle when I'm nervous.**"

I should have taken Adam on Part Two instead of Monica. Adam never giggles!

"There's Max," I whispered.

Monica covered her mouth to muffle her laugh as Max jogged by our hiding place.

"Did you see that?" I asked.

"What?" Monica looked puzzled. She looked around.

"Max is wearing new basketball shoes!" I stepped out of hiding. The new shoes added to the evidence against Max. **They looked really expensive.**

It was time for PART THREE. "Let's follow him," I said.

"Okay," Monica said.

I didn't want to get CAUGHT tailing our suspect, so we stayed half a block behind Max. He went straight to Anna's house and rang the doorbell.

Monica and I crept toward the house behind a tall bush. Then we hid in the bushes by the porch.

When Ben opened the door, we peeked over the porch railing.

"Hey, Max," Ben said. **He looked really excited.** "My new *Viper Man* game is so cool. You're going to be sorry you bought shoes instead. Come on in."

Max did not go inside. He spun around and saw us watching. "Are you following me?" he yelled.

Monica shook her head and giggled. She was too scared to answer. **I froze, but I wasn't afraid.** Ben had just given me clues.

It took a few seconds to sort out the facts.

1. Max didn't know about the zipped pocket in Anna's shoulder bag. So he didn't know she kept her money there.

2. Ben had told Max he couldn't buy the new Viper Man game until he got paid for mowing lawns on Saturday. It was only Thursday. Ben hadn't been paid yet.

"Did you steal Anna's money, Ben?" I blurted out.

"No! I didn't steal it," Ben said. **His face turned red.** He was EMBARRASSED and GUILTY. "I just borrowed the money so I could get the *Viper Man* game a couple days sooner."

Anna's brother Ben did it! I had **solved the case!** Just like a real detective!

"I'm going to pay Anna back," Ben said. "On Saturday."

I gasped. "But Saturday will be too late! Anna needs her money for the Book Fair on Friday," I explained.

"That's tomorrow," Monica said.

"But I won't have ten dollars until Saturday," Ben said.

"Anna is going to be so mad," I said.

"Please don't tell her," Ben pleaded. "She'll tell my parents, and they'll FREAK. I can't pay Anna back if I'm grounded and can't mow lawns."

"But Anna told everyone at school that Monica and I took her money," I said. **"If you don't tell her, everyone will think we are thieves! Forever!"**

CHAPTER 9

THE QUIZ SHOW

Anna was already at her desk when I got to homeroom Friday morning.

"Are you ready for the Quiz Show, Claudia?" she asked.

I wasn't thinking about the Quiz Show. I was thinking about what to say to Anna.

I had practiced what to say over and over in my mind, but there's **NO good way** to tell someone that **her brother is a thief.**

I took a deep breath. "Ben took your ten dollars," I said.

"I know," Anna said. "He told me last night."

I blinked. "He did?"

Anna nodded. "He's going to buy me the book I wanted at the book store tomorrow. **And he's going to get me the next one, too.**"

The bell rang, and I went to my desk. I was so excited I could hardly sit still. I was sure Anna would tell everyone that the thief wasn't Monica or me.

But Anna didn't say anything.

After homeroom, I walked to first period with Monica.

"Shouldn't we tell Anna about Ben?" Monica asked.

I didn't tell Monica that Anna already knew Ben took the money. I didn't want to upset her before the Quiz Show. Besides, I was still hoping Anna would do the right thing and tell the truth.

I pretended I didn't hear the question. Then I gave Monica five dollars.

"What's this?" Monica asked.

"Half the money I made for walking a dog," I said. "I only needed five dollars. Is that enough for you to get the White Pony book?"

"Oh, my gosh, yes!" Monica grinned. "I have three dollars left after buying my sister's birthday present. This is exactly what I need. **Thank you so much.** I'll pay you back soon."

"Okay. You're welcome," I said.

The subject of money didn't come up again until history class.

Ms. Stark had moved the desks into four groups. Each section was marked with colored paper. Monica, Becca, and I joined Anna and Carly by the Green Team sign.

Jenny Pinski stood in front of the Red Team. She folded her arms and frowned. She probably thought she could scare the rest of us into losing.

That wouldn't work. Everyone wanted to see Bad Dog in concert.

Adam and Peter gave each other a high five. The Blue Team still had the best chance to win.

Sylvia was the last person to join her group. She wasn't the only reason I was glad I wasn't on the White Team.

Brad Turino was on the White Team, too. **Brad is really nice for a gorgeous sports star.** But I get totally tongue-tied when I'm around him.

You can't win a Quiz Show if you can't talk.

Anna looked at Monica. "I have to tell you something," she said. "I know that Ben took the money. I promised Ben I wouldn't tell our parents. He's paying me back."

Monica whispered in my ear, "I think Anna was just too EMBARRASSED to admit she was wrong."

"Maybe," I said, "but let's not hold a grudge. Everyone knows we're INNOCENT now. And we'll never see Bad Dog in person if we don't win the Quiz Show."

"Good point," Monica said.

Then Ms. Stark went over the Quiz Show rules.

"The team that hits the buzzer first answers the question," Ms. Stark explained. "That team will get five points for a **correct** answer."

"What if the answer is WRONG?" Peter asked.

"The other **three teams** will write down their answer," Ms. Stark said. "Every team that answers correctly will get five points."

"Okay, Greens." Anna held up her hand. We all slapped it for luck. "Let's go for it!" Anna yelled.

Ms. Stark had a jar full of folded papers. She pulled ONE OUT.

"The first question is: Justice in the United States is based on what principle?" She asked.

I hit the buzzer 𝔽𝕀ℝ𝕊𝕋 and answered.

"Everyone is innocent until proven guilty."

CHAPTER 10

P.S.

Everyone **felt bad** for accusing me and  Monica of taking Anna's money.

I won't blame anyone for anything without proof ever again.

Mr. Gomez bugged me about finding the dog that messed up his yard. He asked me about it every day for a week!

I DIDN'T LIE about it exactly. **I just didn't say anything.**

The morning messes stopped, so he finally stopped asking.

I walked Buster on different streets so Mr. Gomez wouldn't see us.

- 76 -

After Mrs. Arnold's son got back, Mrs. Arnold gave me an **extra five dollars.** She promised to call me whenever she needed a dog-walker.

And as I expected, the Blue Team won the Quiz Show.

Everyone on the Green Team WON a  dollar-off coupon at the book fair for coming in second.

But that wasn't the best part. Adam, Peter, and Tommy each **won two Bad Dog tickets. So they took Monica, Becca, and me to the concert with them!**

And Jenny Pinski didn't stomp anyone on the Red Team.

The End

About the Author

Diana G. Gallagher lives in Florida with her husband and five dogs, four cats, and a cranky parrot. Her hobbies are gardening, garage sales, and grandchildren. She has been an English equitation instructor, a professional folk musician, and an artist. However, she had aspirations to be a professional writer at the age of twelve. She has written dozens of books for kids and young adults.

About the Illustrator

Brann Garvey grew up in the great state of Iowa, where he studied art and visual communications. He graduated from the Minneapolis College of Art and Design with a degree in illustration. Brann is usually found with one or more of the following: a pencil in his hand, a comic book, a remote for watching DVDs, or his pet kitty, Iggy. When the weather is nice, Brann likes to play disc golf, and he proudly points out that Iowa is one of the world's centers for the sport. Iggy does not play.

Glossary

accused (uh-KYOOZD)—if a person is accused of doing something, someone else thinks that they have done it

arrest (uh-REST)—to put someone in jail

circumstantial evidence (sur-kum-STAN-shuhl EV-uh-duhnss)—evidence that doesn't prove an idea

commit (kuh-MIT)—to do something wrong

evidence (EV-uh-duhnss)—information or facts that help prove something

guilty (GIL-tee)—to have committed a crime

innocent (IN-uh-suhnt)—not guilty

means (MEENZ)—the ability to do something

motive (MOH-tiv)—a reason for doing something

opportunity (op-ur-TOO-nuh-tee)—a chance

reasonable doubt (REE-zuhn-uh-buhl DOUT)—if you have reasonable doubt, you are not convinced

reward (ree-WOHRD)—something you receive for doing something good or helpful

verdict (VUR-dikt)—a decision

witness (WIT-niss)—someone who has seen something

Discussion Questions

1. Have you ever been accused of something you didn't do? How did it make you feel? How did you resolve the situation? Talk about what happened and other ways you could have handled it.

2. In this book, Claudia is on a team for the Quiz Show. Sometimes teams work well together, but sometimes they don't. How do you think Claudia's team worked together? What are some other things they could have done to work together as a team? What are some ways that you have worked with a team? Talk about what it means to be a good teammate.

3. On page 75, Claudia says that everyone is innocent until proven guilty. What does that mean? Talk about it.

Writing Prompts

1. Claudia has more than one best friend. Write a short description of one of your closest friends. What does he or she look like? Where does he or she live? What kind of things does he or she like to do for fun?

2. Do you have bad luck, good luck, or (like Claudia) even luck? Write about what kind of luck you think you have, and don't forget to give examples from your life!

3. Claudia needs to save money for the Book Fair. She comes up with some ways to make money. Brainstorm some other ways she could have earned the money she needed. What would you do, if you needed to earn money? Make a list.

MORE FUN
with Claudia!

Claudia Cristina Cortez

Just like every other thirteen-year-old girl, Claudia Cristina Cortez has a complicated life. Whether she's studying for the big Quiz Show, babysitting her neighbor, Nick, avoiding mean Jenny Pinski, planning the seventh-grade dance, or trying desperately to pass the swimming test at camp, Claudia goes through her complicated life with confidence, cleverness, and a serious dash of cool.

Meet

David Mortimore Baxter

David is a great kid, but he has one big problem — he can't stop talking. These wildly humorous stories, told by David himself, will show you just how much trouble a boy and his mouth can get into, whether he's making promises to become class president or bragging that he's best friends with the world's most famous wrestler. David is fun, engaging, cool, and smart enough to realize that growing up is the biggest adventure of all.

Do you want to know more about subjects related to this book? Or are you interested in learning about other topics? Then check out FactHound, a fun, easy way to find Internet sites.

Our investigative staff has already sniffed out great sites for you!

Here's how to use FactHound:

1. Visit *www.facthound.com*

2. Select your grade level.

3. To learn more about subjects related to this book, type in the book's ISBN number: **159889840X**.

4. Click the **Fetch It** button.

FactHound will fetch the best Internet sites for you!